SHEDDING SKINS

SHEDDING SKINS

BRAIN JAR PRESS Short Fiction Lab #5

PETER M. BALL

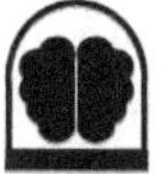

ISBN: 978-0-6481761-7-6 (Print)

A Brain Jar Press Book
www.brainjarpress.com

SHEDDING SKINS

The veranda won't last the summer. The warped are rotting in places, leaving jagged gaps where you can see the dust and spider webs underneath. Mariah tries to keep herself busy, makes small repairs around the decaying edges: A gleaming silver knocker amid the flaking paint of the front door; Purple velvet replacing the ratty curtains. Doing the best she can with the supplies we brought, knowing that it's futile.

I claim the veranda as my domain. Through the languid daylight hours, I sit on a faded canvas chair, surrounding myself with plumes of cigarette smoke and empty teacups. Occasionally, Mariah will stop by, pausing her steady stream of home improvements to check on me. She pretends she is no longer concerned by the tremor as I hand-roll my tobacco, or my intent fascination with the fence line between our overgrown yard and the neighbor's close-cropped sheep paddock. I pretend to be okay with her keeping busy, despite the orders to take it easy and rest.

As night creeps up on us, Mariah takes her chances

sitting on the balcony rail. We roll a joint, open a bottle of wine, struggle to find something we can discuss without devolving into an argument. The pot dries the mouth, it's flavor washed away by sweat and a glass of terrible red. Sometimes I forget why Mariah agreed to move to a rundown house six hundred kilometers from home, or how we'd both grown comfortable with silence as our default state. I'll reach across to trace the line of the scar through the patchy stubble on her scalp. Her skin crawls at the contact, and I remember where we are and why we've come.

I whisper, "Sorry," and Mariah murmurs a tired response. My apology is meaningless, and we both recognize its futility beyond offering a comforting ritual. Contrition is hard to manage out here, with the empty sky and the heat-haze. Mariah sits, quietly brooding.

In bed I reach out for her, attempting to bridge the distance. The cicadas sing, their steady hum comforting in the darkness. Sweat coats us both, makes us slick against one another.

Here, at least, Mariah struggles with me in the fight to reconnect. "Harley, It's okay," she whispers. "We'll figure it out, I promise."

Late at night, when I'm trying to doze, I can hear them slithering beneath the floorboards. An audible rasp of scale on scale discernible in every pause of Mariah's rumbling snore.

When I sleep, my dreams are without form, meaningless montages of movement and instinct and the taste of prey on the wind. Half-remembered sequences of coil and strike and swallow, the heavy weight of digesting mice lodged in my stomach.

When the morning sun forces its way past Mariah's

curtains, the dim light battling the velvet, the aftertaste of that formless hunt lingers on my tongue. Poison. Terror. A creature, soft and small and warm, pressed against the membranes.

The sensation haunts me until breakfast's over and I spark up my first cigarette of the day, using nicotine and burning flame to scour away the unsettling memory.

The python's lurking when I step onto the balcony, a dull presence that tugs on the fringes of my vision. Mariah is working at the kitchen table, threading twine through holes drilled in scavenged debris. I can hear her, taste her perfume lingering in the air, the subtle blend of sweat and musty sugar.

I take my position on the chair as though nothing is wrong, light a cigarette and feign ignorance about the snake's presence. Focus my attention on the sheep, the faint wisps of cloud gathering on the very edge of the horizon. Mariah working inside the flat, and the sound of wind passing over the long grass. The occasional semi-trailer thundering across the distant highway, engine noise drifting over kilometres of ewes, rams, and staggered barbed wire fence line.

We'd discussed the inevitability of encountering snakes, Mariah and I. Discussed it and my phobias, when we saw overgrown yard and sparse gum trees, after Mariah noted the faint skitter of mice and bush-rats playing among the corrugated roof and the cluttered debris stored under the house.

I tremor at the thought of the snake these days, my resilience worn down long before we rolled off a highway. An irrational fear born of childhood, my father keeping carpet snakes as pets in heated cages lined with wood chips. My dad allowed me to name the mice he bought, before they became snake food.

My phobia lingered well after my father passed on. A paralysing fear that once saw me carried out of the reptile house of the San Diego Zoo, paralysed with panic and weeping. Unable to face the prospect of encountering a cobra or black mamba secured behind thick glass, always afraid of being eaten and the long, slow process of digestion.

Mariah fretted about my ability to cope with the bush, and I assured her I had it under control. That I could contain the fear of a scaled form dropping on me from the trees, or sliding into bed and finding a serpent coiled around my feet. I promised Mariah I could handle encountering a red belly or carpet python out in the grass.

And it surprises me, when I succumb to the lure of the serpent's presence, to discover I wasn't lying.

Its sleek form draped over the peeling railings, a black stain against the dust-streaked cream paint. The snake holds its head high, staring at me, tasting the air with its tongue. I can't place the breed, and that bothers me. There's so many snakes out here, endless venomous threats with no reason to trust humans, and we're so far from a hospital.

I suck it up and make the best of it. "Morning," I say, my voice steady. No sweat, no pounding pulse, no twinge of fear in my stomach. The snake watches, and I stare back, wondering when the fear will come.

It hisses; a soft rasp that slices through me the same way as Mariah unleashing an irritated sigh. Then, with slow and deliberate poise, the serpent bares its fangs and the fear sets in.

My hand spasms, trembling. I can see the glowing tip of the cigarette dancing at the edge of my vision. It takes three attempts to get it in my mouth, to inhale the smoke and calm the sudden leap in my lungs. I count out the distance between me and the snake, calculate the time required for it to untangle from the struts and cover the twelve feet between its perch and mine.

It flicks out a tongue, looks smug when it tastes fear in the air. Then its black length disappears, sliding through a cracked floorboard. I'm alone on the veranda, listening to Mariah working and the quick tattoo of my pulse.

We hear the semi-trailers roaring as we eat, their call whisper-soft after drifting across the paddocks. I cling to the sounds as best I can, the faint reminder of civilization giving me a moment of comfort. Mariah focuses on dinner with grim determination, excluding all else. She eats mechanically, counting the number of times she needs to chew before swallowing. In the lull between road trains the emptiness stretches out, poised and full of danger.

"There was a snake today," I tell her. "Out on the veranda."

Mariah swallows before nodding.

"He finally relocated then," she says.

"From where?" I ask, but there's no answer except her silent chewing. I join her countdown, patiently waiting for her to reach zero and swallow. She wipes the side of her face with a sleeve.

"Poor guys been hiding out in the wreckage downstairs." Mariah chases a fresh spoonful of peas and corn across her plate, unconcerned with the note of panic in my voice.

"You think it's safe rummaging around down there with a snake about?"

"No. But nothing's safe anymore." Mariah scooped another mouthful and chewed. Already bored with the topic, retreating into routine. The snake is the first thing she's engaged with since we arrived, the first real conversation we've had involving monosyllables.

I squelch my fear long enough to attempt a fresh tactic: "How do you know it's a male?"

The spoonful of peas stalls halfway to Mariah's mouth.

"I just know," she says. "I've known since we've arrived."

They're the last words she speaks for the evening.

Mariah is fast asleep, curled up into a fetal ball that excludes the outside world. I turn off the light and slide in next to her, trying to get comfortable in the oppressive heat. Mariah sleeps easily, despite the silence. I strain to pick up the sound of cars and televisions. Audible signs of life that aren't Mariah and I, or the creatures of the bush.

I notice the snake as my eyes adapt to the darkness, a coiled shadow draped over the eaves outside our window that slowly congeals into something more. There's a glimpse of moonlight on scales, the forked tongue flicking into the night air. It can taste our presence in the room, unfurls and stretches to peer through the cracked glass.

Mariah twitches in her sleep, the unexpected contact between her flesh and mine sending a jolt of panic up my spine. I twist away, heart hammering. She settles back into the mattress. It's a few seconds before I realize that she's awake, her dark eyes open and staring towards the window.

"Babe—"

Mariah knows what's coming. "It's not even poisonous. Ignore it."

"It's watching us," I tell her. "That's not good."

"If it wanted to be in here, neither of us could stop it. It's just soaking up the residual heat in the correlated iron."

That makes sense, and I almost buy it. "But what if it's not?"

The snake hisses and Mariah uncurls, stretches across the bed for the first time in months. I can make out the pale line of her scar as she pulls herself free of the thin blanket.

"It's just singing," she says, falling back against the pillow. "Go to sleep."

I close my eyes and attempt to ignore my beating hard, focusing on my breathing. Mariah hums a lullaby, soft as a whisper, until the dream begin.

The scar tissue on Mariah's head is because of the accident. We rolled our car on the way back from Sydney, spent three days in the Lismore hospital while she recovered from the impact. My injuries were comparatively minor, anxiety compounded by my irritation at making a stupid mistake and the consequences that followed.

The scar tissue of our hearts existed long before the wreck. They're the product of the slow drift apart, the mistakes made as we tried to close the gap or fill the aches it caused.

We decided to try again, bail on our lives, and revisit the family homestead. Nobody there but here and me, waiting to rediscover the things we used to love in the other person. Or discover something new, out in my grandmother's house, long neglected and ignored by the rest of my siblings. Rent-free living, in exchange for what renovations we could handle, an attempt to gussy the old place up well enough to sell.

Buying time to reinvent ourselves as a couple. Or simply reinvent ourselves into people who might be capable of living apart.

All or nothing, Mariah called it. We come home together or kill each other.

On Tuesday morning, the radio warns us of storms. I spend the day studying the horizon and the rain edging in over the hills. Mariah joins me after the announcement, leans the faded denim of her jeans against the peeling paint of the railing. I watch the back of her head, the thin line of her scar beneath the blonde.

"Looks nasty," she says, and her voice is hollow. The storm changes the atmosphere, subtle shifts in wind and temperature occurring long before the downpour arrives.

"Three hours until it hits," I tell her. "Maybe four."

The heat of the day gets worse, the air getting thicker as we wait. Mariah works in the yard, cutting back overgrown grass, tying the withering remains of a tomato vine to the fence. In the midday swelter her skin gleams, the faint patina of sweat shining, fluid and slippery. Her body twists and bends, fingers weaving through the fencing wire as she threads the twine.

The rain reaches the property after lunch, gets heavier as the afternoon wears us down. We break open the last bottle of scotch brought from the city, swilling the musty taste around in our mouths as the torrential downpour hits the earth. The world is darker, the air thick with falling raindrops. I lose sight of the fence, everything outside shrinking away until I'm left with the veranda, the house, Mariah and the storm. She sits with her legs crossed, back against the pale wood slats of the wall. I offer her a cigarette, watch her draw one with fingers stained by dirt and arms red with nettle stings. After she lights up, Mariah peels grass seeds and burrs from her jeans. She picks at the frayed hole in the denim above her right knee.

Through the grey haze of the downpour, lightning flashes. "The kitchen will be leaking," Mariah says. She pauses, breathes deeply against the cigarette. "And the bathroom."

I nod. Pour scotch into the frosted plastic mugs we found among the ruins of the pantry. She holds it up, considers it carefully before putting it to her lips. Her eyes dangerously flat. A question looms, sits on the tip of our tongues, but Mariah doesn't give it voice and I don't have the heart. What hangs between us isn't quite silence, but it's an mute conversation fighting to conquer the rumble of the storm. The house struggles to stay aloof from its surroundings, creaking in the wind.

I touch her arm. For the first time in days Mariah doesn't pull back, doesn't shrink from contact. Our lips and tongues find one-another, fingers clawing, a fierce embrace. The passion burns fast, then splutters out. A moment of respite, done and forgotten.

Mariah retreats, and my hands shake as I pour a fresh mug, spilling scotch onto the dusty floorboards.

Silence wakes me before dawn. I listen to the absences, waiting for the sound of the storm to return. The house has stopped creaking in the wind, the corrugated iron roof no longer rattling with under the impact of falling raindrops. The absence echoes. Nothing.

When I open my eyes, Mariah is sitting by the window. Her face is pale, milky in the dim light. I watch her lips moving, a silent prayer into the darkness. There are no words, just the soft hiss and click of her mouth, her tongue against her teeth as sibilant noises form beneath her breath.

I prop myself up on the pillows, stretch to catch her attention. Mariah ignores me, focused on the window. Keeps muttering, concentrating. There are stars out, patches of night sky previously hidden. Her scar is a jagged line in the moonlight, easily visible against the pale gleam of her hair. Along the horizon, a seam of amber and red. Pre-dawn struggling against the clouds.

"Morning?"

Mariah's lips stop moving, lock shut. The smile she offers holds no emotion, it's an adornment worn for my benefit. In the dim light, her eyes are empty and black.

"You're awake," she says, then pauses, her expression clouded by half-light and shadow. "Good."

A grimy ray of sunlight struggles through the velvet curtains, sheds its radiance on the litter of sweat-stained clothes and rumpled sheets kicked off during the night. There are floorboards in the bedroom, ancient wood that creaks with each deliberate step Mariah takes. She slips into the bed, under the summer sheet that barely protects us from the mosquitoes. She leans in, places her forehead against mine. Her skin cool in the humid air.

"Good," she says again, but her voice is empty. Distant. Her breathing light and steady, warm against my face. A callous finger tracing the line of my cheek. The delicate flick of her tongue tasting my upper lip. Her body coils around me, her head nestling against my neck. My arms hold her by instinct. I'm frightened of my warmth, burning against her flesh.

"I couldn't sleep," she tells me. "Bad dreams."

And her calm breathing fills my ears.

The distracting itch begins the day after the storm. At first, faint irritation that drifts around my body with the blood and oxygen. A mild annoyance, only truly noticed in the idle periods between cigarettes and scratching. Mariah nods when I tell her, resumes her task of planting seeds in the warm mud by the fence.

By mid afternoon I have red marks on my chest, and I'm peeling flakes of dry flesh off my arms and legs. I switch to chamomile tea and my left hand shakes holding up the chipped saucer to catch drips. For the first time that I can remember, my eyelid itches.

"Sunburn," Mariah tells me.

I close my eyes and try to believe her. She's the one who spends time out in the sun, not me.

Mariah finds the moulted snakeskin just before sunset, entwined around the low edge of a fence post amongst the tangle of weeds. I watch her from the veranda, scratching as she leans forward to touch it. Her knees squelch in the mud and grass, her hand barely brushing the translucent surface before she recoils. She clenches the hand to her chest, rubs at the fingertips with her thumb.

I roll tobacco as she reaches out again. The crumpled skin is stronger than it looks, able to withstand her touch. Mariah smiles and untangles it from the fence. She hums as she does so, a sound just loud enough to catch on the breeze. I finish my cigarette and she pulls it free, cradling the empty weight in curved fingers. She stares at the dead husk in her hands, her eyes shining.

"Carpet snake," she calls out. "Common around these parts. Mostly harmless."

The snake we've encountered isn't a carpet python. Nothing so harmless.

Still, when I don't answer Mariah brings the sloughed-off skin to me. Climbing the steps she holds it forward, an offering, waiting for me to touch. The pale sepia of flesh that has outlived its usefulness terrifies me. I try to avoid thoughts of the snake itself, lurking beyond the fence line among the tangle of sheep-paddock and scrub, acquainting itself with a fresh layer of scales.

I can hear the rasping whisper on the wind.

"Impressive," I tell her and Mariah thrusts the snake-skin forward again, gestures for me to touch it. My flesh crawls, clammy with fear. I scramble, trying to get away.

Mariah shrugs. She sits on the front steps and hums to herself, examining the husk, tipping it back and forth in exploratory curiosity. She runs her hands along the length of it, delicate and tender. When she's done, she looks at me over her shoulder. Her face animated, her eyes shining.

"It won't hurt you," Mariah tells me. "It's just shed scales. No more dangerous than your sunburn."

I keep my eyes on the fence. Silence stretches out, filling the veranda, the yard, the paddock beyond. I light another cigarette, a defence against the awkwardness. Mariah smiles, wraps the skin around her neck with exaggerated care. When it's in place, she stands over me. Holds the dead scales as though the snake were alive, an exotic dancer's pet, and she sways. Softly. Slowly. Her arms gleaming with sweat. The line of her belly, tanned and inviting, where her jeans and shirt don't meet.

"Look," she says. Her voice is low, the hint of a suggestion.

I don't.

"Can you throw it away? Please?"

Mariah blinks. Stops swaying and nods. When she moves, her steps are tentative. Her eyes are flat again, the distraction gone. She pets the snakeskin and retreats.

Later I find it tacked to the door of the toilet, its length dangling from the top of the frame to the floor. I remember my itching skin, suddenly aware of how tight and awkward flesh feels when stretched over sinew, muscle, and bone. Afraid of all the hidden things finally bursting free.

I take to urinating off the edge of the veranda so I don't have to deal with the skin.

Three days after the storm, I stop eating meat. It begins with breakfast, when a sausage is suddenly thick and wooly in my mouth. I chew doggedly, trying to ignore the texture of dust and dry fur. My teeth click and scrape, ominously loud in my ears. Mariah smiles and slices her sausages neatly, devouring each morsel with delicate care. My second bite is worse than the first, like trying to swallow something alive. I try washing the third under the spluttering tap to ensure it's clean.

I leave my next sausage uneaten on the plate. Mariah throws it to the magpies and heads outside, starting work on the junk underneath the house. At dinner I sniff the hamburger patties, testing them with the tip of my tongue. They're warm and living, soft to touch. I lose my appetite.

I eat out on the veranda, nibbling at a frayed and decaying lettuce leaf. Dipping chunks of browning apple into leftover scotch, savoring the heady scent and the wood smoke flavor it brings to the fruit. When our wilting fruit and vegetables no longer meet my needs, I survive the rest of the day eating toast with thin scrapings of Vegemite and butter.

Mariah's content to let me hoard our vegetables, starts gorging on meat with a carnivore's enthusiasm. She sits at the kitchen table, cutting steaks and sausages into small morsels that she launches into the air and catches in her mouth. Mariah barely chews before swallowing, patiently slicing the next morsel free.

We stop sharing meals. We speak only when necessary, our voices muted and husky from too much silence. At times, Mariah will sing, half-remembered snatches of songs that emerge tuneless and monotone. When I try to join her, Mariah falls silent. A hiss in the soft shadow of her breath.

Occasionally the same tune echoes underneath the house, a siren's song drifting up through the holes in the floor.

We didn't bring sufficient floorboards to repair the broken wood, so I give the damage a wide berth. My gut tells me no good will come from straying too close to those depths, trying to seek the source of our music.

This isn't her. It isn't me. The bush is getting to us.

The snakeskin disappears in the night, in the scant hours that Mariah spends sleeping.

She isn't sure if I have something to do with it, blames me out of necessity. After everything that's happened, we've destroyed the trust that once existed. I destroyed it, with bad choices, long before the accident. Mariah no longer knows what I'm truly capable of. During counselling, she confessed to a lingering fear I wrecked our car on purpose. "Easier than living with the guilt," she said.

I told her I wasn't that smart.

So the snakeskin is hardly our first argument, but it's the first since we left the city. We keep our voices soft, even; years of practice have trained us both in the art of using rationalism and calm language as deadly weapons. We let our words twist around each other, looking for openings, ready to strike. Veiled threats and cutting jibes are the only fight we need out here, where melodrama vanishes into the emptiness of the sky.

It takes days to say we're sorry. I'm surprised that Mariah says it first.

Mariah doesn't renovate while she's fuming, and I've given up on the task already. My fortification of the veranda is complete, barricades erected by the detritus of my long occupation. Cigarette butts, empty glasses, the pungent smell of weed and idleness. Mariah spends her time in old enamel bath, soaks in tepid water that leaves her skin gleaming and warm. Occasionally I dart into the kitchen, searching for a cup of tea or a fresh matchstick. There are gifts for me, hidden in nooks and crannies where I stumble over them by accident. A quintet of snake fangs, bound with twine. The fine bones of a serpent's skull. The color illustration of a striking viper, torn from the pages of a children's encyclopedia found in one of the spare bedrooms. When I pass the bathroom, I can hear her talking, hissing beneath her breath.

I promise myself there's nothing to fear in the house, repeat the words as a mantra warding off potential danger.

I pretend the booby traps don't bother me, hold my tongue and circle around them before the fear engulfs me. It's easier to go inside less and less. The sound of Mariah's hiss permeates the walls.

We sleep together, sharing the only bed that still has a mattress and four legs. Mariah's skin is clammy from hours spent in the copper tub. She watches me get changed without speaking. She murmurs to herself while she's sleeping, a constant syllabic whisper with every slow exhalation.

By the time Mariah apologizes, I've given up on the kitchen altogether. The house is a place of danger and silence, traversed with closed eyes, held breath, and prayer. I drink warm beer, stolen from the fridge at dawn and left in the sun all day. Smoke steadily, lighting each cigarette on the dying remnants of the one that came before it. Ignore the twitches of movement among the long grass of the yard, the sound of Mariah talking to herself. I say nothing, do even less, content to hold my position.

The apology, when it comes, is sudden and physical. We're in bed and Mariah's hand slides across my stomach, twining her fingers through mine. My toe runs along the arch of her foot, circling the ankle. Our sorry voiced with the sweaty slide of mouth against body, with searching hands that look for those places where forgiveness is still possible. Anger is an enemy we can overcome with movement and passion, and this time we don't burn out until everything's done and we fall back, breathing hard.

We doze off coiled around one another, sweat staining the sheets. Mariah's breath tickles my ear. The sound of something hissing deep within the house, rising through the cracks.

When I sleep, I dream of poison and scales.

. . .

Morning creeps across the room, light coaxing me into the conscious world. Sheets wrapped around me, coiled into a cotton rope tangled across my neck and torso. I stumble out of bed, my shoulder aching, and head to the bathroom mirror. Bite marks creep their way from arm to collarbone. The product of sharp teeth, pointed, in an almost-human mouth. I wash my injuries and my face, realise too late what's occurred.

The air tastes of dust and sunlight, and Mariah's gone.

Her clothes are strewn across the room, the legacy of her presence tangible through the halls. Snippets of repairs, bundled snake fangs, empty skulls. I reach out and touch the teeth nailed to the kitchen door, running a finger along the fading blue and white twine.

Outside the magpies are launching into the morning chorus, their mangled chortles waking me for the first time in days. The only animal I've heard besides the subliminal hiss caused by hunger and fear. I walk out onto the veranda, inhale the dawn air. Embrace the relief in the warble of magpies, and in my own exhalation, choked and ragged after weeks of smoking.

I cock an ear for Mariah's footsteps or the rustle of movement through the long grass, some indication of the snake is still around.

There's nothing.

I check the rooms, opening the doors by turn. The house is ageing and dangerous, working against exploration. The floors squeak and the door hinges whine. The legacy of Mariah's renovations survive, fresh paint and rich curtains a veneer over the gradual decay. I go room by room: kitchen; bathroom; bedrooms; hallway.

I move on to the space beneath the house, descending with tentative steps. Promising myself there's nothing dangerous among the dirt and forgotten furniture. This is Mariah's domain, the shadowed place she uses to hide and work. I slip between boxes and rusting car parts, the rotting timber of broken tables, chairs, and bedframes. Bypass the skeletons of snakes, dozens of them, nailed to the stout pylons holding the old Queenslander above the earth. Every breath draws in the heady cocktail of dust and mud and fear.

A cool presence coils around my legs, twisting and twining its way across my torso. I hold my breath and wait for the strike, the fangs that will penetrate flesh. There's a twinge in my shoulder, a sharp tang from the bite marks in my skin. For a moment, I can taste Mariah's perfume in the air.

It's there when I emerge into the sunlight, a dull presence that tugs on the fringes of my vision. Black and yellow scales gleam in the morning light, wrapped around the decaying timber on the far end of the veranda. It raises its head to me, bears its fangs by way of greeting. The bite mark on my shoulder twinges again, a pain that spreads across my neck and my chest.

"Mariah?" It seems absurd to say it, but it's the only thing that makes sense to me. We came out here to shed our pasts, and she did. It's so much easier to believe she became a serpent than left me in the night, tramping across the rain-soaked fields to hitch a ride with passing road-trains.

I sit and the snake unfurls, disappears through the hole in the veranda. There's a seam of hardened scales along its skull, a thick line caused by a poorly healed wound.

The python's soft hiss rattles in my ear and I freeze. Refuse to move, long after it slides away.

At sunset I head inside, dig the empty box that holds the snakeskin out of a jumble of boxes hidden in the back of the pantry. It crumples at my touch, flaking off and falling in a shower of petrified snowflakes. It breaks and falls, piece by piece, then sweep the remains into a hole in the floor with the heel of my hand.

I try to start every Short Fiction Lab piece with an experiment—some technique or idea I haven't played with and want to test out in shorter work, or a style I've never attempted before. Other times, they're a matter of looking back and applying different tools. This is one of the latter.

I wrote the earliest versions of Shedding Skin in 2006, the very first short story I drafted when I turned my attention to fiction. The finished draft leant heavily on the techniques brought over from writing poetry—an eye towards the music of the language, and a focus on mood and imagery. It also picked up a lot of positive comments from editors when I started submitting, but never found a home. Mostly, I suspect, because the metaphors didn't land right, and the plot didn't do enough to surprise an experienced reader.

It holds several records from my time sending out short stories—it's had the most requests for rewrites, and some of the longest waits between submission and rejection. Eventually, one magazine sat on a rewrite for two-and-a-half years, and when they finally announced they were folding Shedding Skin felt like an increasingly archaic example of what I could do as a writer. I set it aside for the next fifteen years, consigning it to the trunk story folder.

In the second half of 2019 I tutored in a university course focused on copyediting, spending thirteen weeks talking to emerging editors about tuning up fiction and the difference between proofing work and tightening it. I'd been through copyedits before, but teaching a subject gives you a new appreciation for it value, and shifts your attention in dozens of small ways because you have to figure out how to explain things you take for granted.

Around the same period, I kept getting into discussions about the way artificial intelligence and neural networks could impact writers and editorial processes. One of the biggest potential disruptions out there is the emergence of programs that go a step beyond the spellcheck offered on computers, taking up a lot of the role traditionally occupied by the copyeditor.

A friend of mine urged me to try a prominent AI-editing services out, and I ran *Shedding Skin* through their various reports. The results were... enlightening. I'd expected a slightly more advanced spellcheck, but it highlighted the changes I normally make to a story after I give to my Angela Slatter for the process she dubs 'flensing.'

Essentially, the software showcased the places slowed down by the repetition in words, phrases or structures; all the sentences where I'd lapsed into poor verbiage or distractingly alliterative sequences; and the points where the flow of the story bogged down by heavy introspection.

It's not a substitute for a professional copy edit—at least, not *yet*. It doesn't do context as well as a human would, and therefore misses errors like putting in 2020 instead of 2019 when adding dates to a document.

That said, the software more than proved its value to me as an interim step. It may be slower than an experienced copyeditor, and less prone to picking up small nuances, but I can definitely see its benefit if you're time rich and money poor. It's similarly useful as a tool to flag things a tired reader might miss—or to minimize the hours a human copyeditor spends dealing with mechanical problems.

Anything that frees an editor up to focus on more nuanced aspects of craft is a thing I'm keen to embrace.

If you're curious about how big a difference fifteen years and A.I. make, you can download the original pre-edit story for free using this link: https://BookHip.com/RABWMR

Peter Ball
Brisbane, Australia
January 2020

PETER M. BALL is an author, publisher, and RPG gamer whose love of speculative fiction emerged after exposure to *The Hobbit*, *Star Wars*, David Lynch's *Dune*, and far too many games of *Dungeons and Dragons* before the age of 7. He's spent the bulk of his life working as a creative writing tutor, with brief stints as a performance poet, gaming convention organiser, online content developer, non-profit arts manager, GenreCon convenor, and d20 RPG publisher.

He's the author of the Miriam Aster series and the Keith Murphy Urban Fantasy Thrillers, three short story collections, and more stories, articles, poems, and RPG material than he'd care to count. He's the brain-in-charge at Brain Jar Press, and resides in Brisbane, Australia, with his partner and a very affectionate cat.

Peter can be found online at:
www.petermball.com

ALSO BY PETER M. BALL

BRAIN JAR PRESS SHORT FICTION LAB

The Early Experiments

Winged, With Sharp Teeth

8 Minutes Of Usable Daylight

A White Cross Beside A Lonely Road

One Last First Date Before The End Of The World

SHORT STORY COLLECTIONS

The Birdcage Heart & Other Strange Tales

Not Quite The End Of the World Just Yet: Short Stories & Strange Futures

These Strange & Magic Things: Short Stories

KEITH MURPHY URBAN FANTASY THRILLERS

Exile

Frost

Crusade

MIRIAM ASTER NOVELLAS

Horn

Bleed

ESSAYS

You Don't Want To Be Published & Other Things Nobody Tells You When You First Start Writing

www.ingramcontent.com/pod-product-compliance
Lightning Source LLC
Chambersburg PA
CBHW020237120726